TRANSFORMERS
ROBOTS IN DISGUISE

Sideswipe
Versus
Thunderhoof

by John Sazaklis

LITTLE, BROWN AND COMPANY
New York   Boston

Bumblebee

Sideswipe

Strongarm

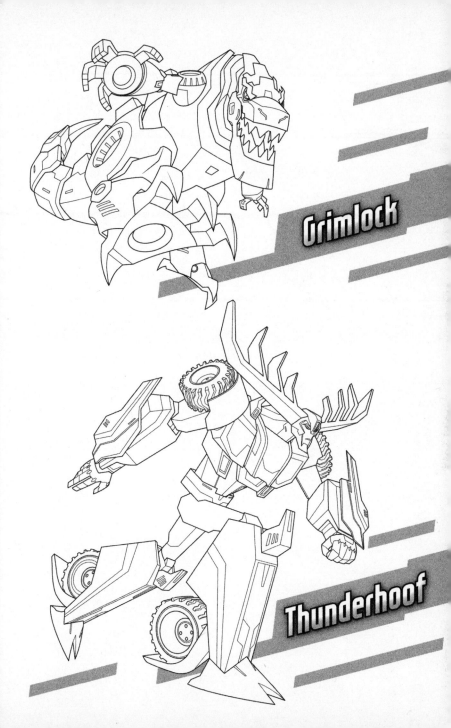

Grimlock

Thunderhoof

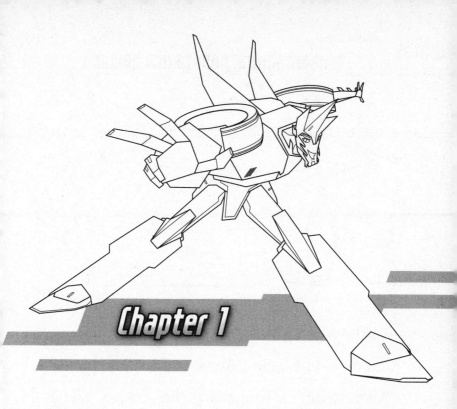

Chapter 1

On the outskirts of Crown City, two vehicles are racing on a secluded, miles-long stretch of road. One is a sleek red sports car, zooming far beyond the legal speed limit. The other, trailing behind, is a blue-and-white police cruiser. Both are more than meets the eye. They are really robots in disguise!

The red sports car is Sideswipe, a fast-talking, fun-loving Autobot from the planet Cybertron. Strongarm, the cruiser, is a young cadet from the Cybertronian Police Force. Both Autobots are members of an elite team that keeps Earth safe from a diabolical faction of robots known as Decepticons.

"Aw, yeah!" cheers Sideswipe as the wind

rushes past him. "This sure beats sitting around the scrapyard."

"*Slow down!*" orders Strongarm.

The hotheaded Autobot disregards the police-bot's command and picks up more speed. Sideswipe and Strongarm are usually at odds with each other. Sideswipe thinks Strongarm is far too serious and hung up on the rules. Strongarm finds Sideswipe's

disregard for order and authority extremely annoying.

The red sports car blasts his radio speakers, filling the air with an earsplitting, guitar-shredding heavy metal song.

"Ack! What an assault on the audio receptors!" Strongarm cries.

"Catch me if you can!" Sideswipe replies. "Or else, eat my dust!"

Sideswipe's tires kick up a cloud of dirt as he barrels faster down the road.

The dust cloud envelops Strongarm, but she does not waver in her course.

"You want to play dirty, Sideswipe? Fine by me," she says. "Eat *this*!"

In an instant, Strongarm shifts from her vehicle mode into her robot form. She

somersaults in the air and lands right on top
of Sideswipe.

THUD!

"Tag, you're it!" she exclaims.

"Hey, watch the paint job!" Sideswipe cries. "Okay, let's see how *strong* you really are!"

The sports car swerves quickly to the left and then veers hard to the right. Strongarm keeps her grip as well as her cool.

"Is that the best you got?" she taunts. "At the academy, we were taught to expect the unexpected."

"We're making an unexpected stop," Sideswipe says. "And this is where you get off!"

The Autobot slams on his brakes, and his tires squeal against the gravel.

SCREEEEE!

Strongarm hurtles forward and lands on the road in front of Sideswipe.

SLAM!

"Oof!" says Strongarm.

Changing from his vehicle mode into his robot form, Sideswipe lends Strongarm a hand and helps her off the ground.

"Are you okay?" he asks.

"My ego is more bruised than anything else. I should have heeded my own advice."

At that moment, the two Autobots feel a low rumble under their feet. There is another vehicle heading their way.

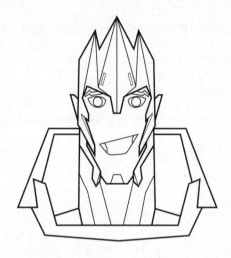

"Speaking of unexpected, who is that?" Sideswipe asks.

Strongarm focuses her ocular sockets on the approaching object. "It appears to be a human inside a regulation pickup truck. Probably a local produce supplier. Quick, we must maintain our cover!"

In the blink of an eye, Strongarm and Sideswipe change back into vehicles. They idle by the side of the road as the farmer's truck approaches them.

"Too bad," Sideswipe laments. "I was kind of hoping it would be a Decepticon, you know? I'm all revved up and ready for action!"

"Throttle back, tough-bot," Strongarm says.

The two Autobots remain silent as the pickup passes by. The bed of the truck is piled high with crates. Each one is stuffed to the brim with vegetables.

Suddenly, the truck's front tire bursts.

BAM!

The driver lets out a cry of alarm as he loses control of the pickup. There is a wrenching sound of metal as the front tires pop off their axis. The crates on the bed of the truck teeter and totter while the vehicle swerves from side to side.

"Whoa!" exclaims Sideswipe. "Who ordered the tossed salad?"

In the distance, another truck is traveling down the same road in the opposite direction.

"Those two vehicles will collide unless we intervene!" Strongarm cries.

"Well, I wanted excitement," Sideswipe replies. "So let's rock and roll!"

Chapter 2

The Autobots rush after the runaway truck.

ZOOOOM!

Within seconds, the two heroes flank the pickup. Strongarm pulls up on the left side, next to the driver. The frightened farmer sees the police cruiser and calms down. He grips the steering wheel and shouts, "Help me!"

As the pickup skids to the right, Sideswipe is there to keep it steady. He winces as the truck scrapes against him. There is a shower of sparks as metal grinds against metal.

SKRRRRRRUNCH!

"Argh! There goes the paint job!" Sideswipe groans.

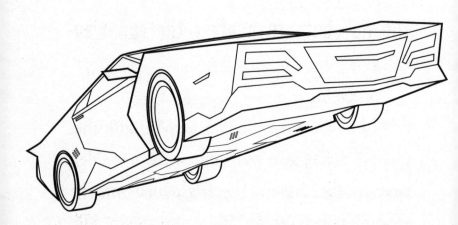

"Focus on the bigger picture," replies Strongarm.

Together, the tenacious teammates try to guide the pickup onto a parallel path while helping decrease its speed. Unfortunately, the oncoming truck and its driver are unaware of the danger that lies ahead.

"That other vehicle isn't slowing down, Sideswipe," Strongarm states. "I'll need you to take point here!"

"Aye, aye, captain!" Sideswipe replies.

Simultaneously, the Autobots peel away from the pickup and speed past it. Sideswipe cuts in front and slows down until his rear bumper touches the truck's grille. Then he pumps his brakes, bringing both himself and the pickup to a complete stop.

Strongarm continues her course, turning on her siren and flashing lights to capture the driver's attention. As the big rig careens closer, she realizes the oncoming vehicle is a fuel truck!

"Oh, scrud!" she exclaims.

The gas tanker is much closer now, and having seen the police cruiser, the driver slams on his brakes. The tires squeal and tear divots into the road. The air fills with dust and the acrid smell of burning rubber, but the truck continues to barrel toward Strongarm—its massive size and weight pushing it forward.

Thinking quickly, the Autobot pivots ninety degrees, bringing her broadside perpendicular to the truck. She braces herself for the impact as Sideswipe watches on in horror.

"Strongarm...NO!" he yells.

SCREEEEEEEEEEEEEECH!

The tanker's brakes emit an ear-piercing squeal as the vehicle grinds to a halt.

Then silence.

When the dust finally settles, Sideswipe realizes that the gas tanker has stopped only inches away from Strongarm. The police cruiser is still in one piece!

Before either Autobot can react, the farmer shouts from his window.

"Thank you so much, whoever you are!"

Then he climbs out of the pickup and walks over to Sideswipe. He tries to peek inside the tinted windows.

BEEP! BEEP!

Strongarm honks her horn, distracting the farmer.

Sideswipe revs his engine and peels out around the pickup and onto the road. Strongarm follows close behind.

The driver of the gas tanker and the bewildered farmer watch as the mysterious sports car and police cruiser disappear along the horizon.

What started as a friendly competition nearly ended in disaster. Sideswipe is relieved that Strongarm is unharmed, but he would rather not admit it to her.

After a long while, Strongarm breaks the silence.

"You know, we kinda work well together," she says.

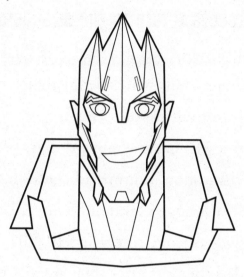

"Yeah, you're right," Sideswipe replies. "But if you tell anyone back at the base that I said that, I'll deny it! I have a reputation to uphold."

"Deal," Strongarm says, and laughs.

The Autobots return to the scrapyard and roll up through two aisles of miscellaneous junk. There, they switch from their vehicle modes into their robot forms.

The Crown City scrapyard has become the new Autobots' command center here on Earth. It belongs to human Denny Clay and his twelve-year-old son, Russell. The Clays befriended the bots after they literally crash-landed into their lives some time ago. They also help the Autobots to track down and capture Decepticon fugitives running amok on Earth.

"Welcome back, bots!" says a friendly voice.

It belongs to Bumblebee, Sideswipe and Strongarm's determined and kindhearted team leader. Bumblebee was the lieutenant of the police force back on Cybertron. Now he is in charge of this ragtag bunch of robots that can sometimes be more trouble than a dozen Decepticons.

"I hope that training exercise helped bring you a little closer to working better together."

"Too close for comfort, if you ask me," Sideswipe says, looking at the scratches on his plating.

"Sideswipe shows great potential, Lieutenant," Strongarm says to Bumblebee. "He just needs to be a little more serious."

"If I get any more serious I'll suffer from brain rust. Or worse...I'll turn into *you*!"

"I can certainly give you more dings, if you like!"

"Keep your optics on the prize, guys," Bumblebee interrupts. "Next training exercise will be centered on the use of our weapons. We all know that they are powerful energy weapons that manifest whatever we need in

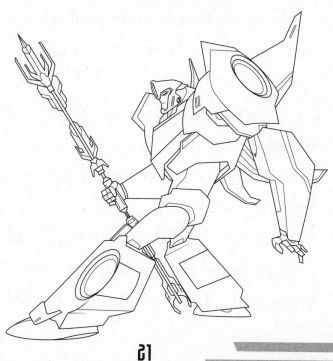

battle just with sheer thought or will. *That's* where your focus counts!"

At that moment, Denny and Russell appear. Denny lets out a long whistle.

"Whoa, Sideswipe, what happened?" he asks. "You really got that authentic 'battle damage' thing going on!"

"Yeah, you look like you went ten rounds with Thunderhoof in the Rumbledome!" Russell adds.

"Thunderhoof?!" Sideswipe exclaims. "That slag-heap doesn't stand a chance against me! Why, I'll turn him into scrap metal the next time I see him!"

"Quit blowing exhaust," Strongarm chides. "We all know that he is a very dangerous Decepticon. And now that he's teamed up with Steeljaw, well, it's enough to give me nightmares for the next ten cycles!"

"Luckily, Steeljaw and his gang have been keeping a low profile," Bumblebee says. "And speaking of, what *really* happened to you?"

Sideswipe smiles. "We had to intervene and help some civilians in trouble. No biggie."

Bumblebee's optics go wide.

"You did *what*?" he exclaims. "By the All-Spark!"

"Relax, Bee," Sideswipe says with a shrug. "Nothing happened. Nobody saw us. We stayed *incognito* the whole time!"

Bumblebee always worries about keeping their presence unknown to humans, but Denny and Russell are exceptions that he's made.

"I've got some touch-up paint," Denny offers. "We can buff the plating out, wax it up, and make you brand-new."

"Sounds like a good time to me," Sideswipe says. "Thanks!"

"Change of plans, team," Bumblebee says. "I just got a message from the command center: *Intruder alert!*"

Chapter 3

In rapid succession, Bumblebee and his team shift from their bot modes into vehicles. Strongarm takes Denny as her passenger, and Sideswipe scoops up Russell.

Together, they race toward the command center—a part of the scrapyard that has become their new base of operations.

Amid the control panels, two more members of Team Bee are intently watching the computer screen. They are the smallest and biggest bots at the yard.

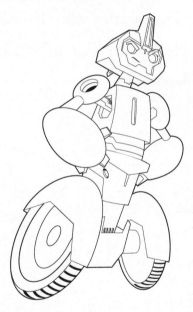

The little one is Fixit. This multitasking mini-con was pilot of the prison transport ship *Alchemor*—the same ship that crashed to Earth and let loose the countless Decepticon criminals. Now he serves as the resident handy-bot and lookout.

The big bot is Grimlock. He is a dinobot and former Decepticon who defected to the Autobots. He's really not a bad bot—he's just misunderstood.

"Intruder dessert...avert...alert!" Fixit cries.

The crash left him with a slight malfunction. After a quick chuck, Fixit rights himself once again. "I've prepared the defense systems. Shall I activate them?"

The Autobots change back and crowd around the mini-con.

"Not just yet," Bumblebee replies. "Allow me to get a closer look."

The lieutenant studies the screen and finds three individuals lurking around the perimeter of the scrapyard. They are wearing tattered clothing held together with safety pins. The one in front is covered in tattoos and has a buzzed head.

"Hmm. They appear to be battle-ravaged,"

Bumblebee states. "One of them is marked with curious and indecipherable symbols. If we scan them into the holo-scroll we can find out if they are a threat or not."

"They could be the human versions of Decepticons," Sideswipe jokes. "They look like bad guys."

Bumblebee shoots Sideswipe a stern look.

"These beings do indeed look unsavory," Strongarm agrees.

"They don't look so bad to me," says Grimlock. "Maybe they're nice?"

Bumblebee ruminates for a moment. The dinobot has a point.

"Grimlock is right," he says. "We shouldn't be so quick to judge. After all, appearances *can* be deceiving."

Denny lets out a belly laugh, startling the group.

"Need I remind you that you're all robots in disguise?"

Russell pushes his way toward the screen.

"I know them," he says with a scowl.

"What are they?" Strongarm implores.

"They're *teenagers*. And they're my class-mates."

A wave of disbelief passes over the Auto-bots.

"Clearly, they've repeated the grade a few times," Russell adds.

"Wow!" Sideswipe exclaims. "They must think school is really cool."

"No. They think they *rule* the school," Russell replies.

"Ha!" Strongarm scoffs. "They wouldn't last a day in the academy."

Fixit fidgets nervously.

"Best not to take any chimps . . . champs . . . chances!" the mini-con stammers.

"The little bot is right! Time for an inter-rogation!" Sideswipe shouts gleefully.

"Hey, I give the orders around here,

remember?" Bumblebee interjects. "Fixit, stand down. They are civilians."

Bumblebee turns to Sideswipe.

"When I asked you to step up your game on the team I didn't intend for you to skip the line straight to leader."

"What can I say, Bee? I'm an overachiever."

Bumblebee cannot help but smile in spite of himself.

"Maybe they're customers," Denny says hopefully.

Bumblebee nods. "Come on, Autobots, let's let Denny and Russell conduct their business as usual."

The bots shift into their vehicle modes and pull into parking spots in a small lot full of used cars. Fixit hides under a large trash can, and Grimlock tries to look as inconspicuous as possible by freezing in place.

The humans hurry toward the front entrance of the scrapyard.

"This'll be a blast and a half, Rusty," Denny says to his son. "I've never met any of your school friends before."

"It's Russell, Dad. And they're not my friends," Russell says, correcting his father. "They're my classmates. And they're all jerks."

The twelve-year-old falls silent as they walk along. It was true his father was not around much when he was growing up. Now, with his mom traveling in Europe, Russell was spending a lot more time with his dad.

In the distance, the three teens climb onto a rusted and bent highway sign and slide down into another clearing in the yard. They whoop and holler at their newfound diversion.

"Those kids could get hurt doing that," Denny says.

Russell rolls his eyes.

"Stay here, Dad. Let me handle this."

Russell walks over to his classmates. The tallest one notices him first.

"Yo, Joey! Johnny! Look who it is!"

Joey, the red-haired one with glasses, squints at Russell and sneers.

"Well, if it isn't little Rusty Clay," he says.

"It's Russell," the boy replies.

Johnny, the black-haired one with a stubbly beard, ambles over. He's wiping dirt off his ripped jeans.

"From the looks of this place, we should call him Dusty Clay! *Ha!*"

"Nice one, Johnny," Joey says. "Didja hear that, Steve? *Dusty* Clay! Ha!

The two friends high-five each other.

Steve, the tall one with the tattoos and a buzzed head, steps up and looks down at Russell.

"What brings *you* to *our* new hangout, Dusty?" he asks.

"Hate to break it to you, *Stevie*, but it's *my* hangout," Russell replies.

Steve blinks in surprise.

"Is that so, small fry?" he taunts. "What if I say it's mine now?"

He shoves Russell to the ground.

A deep voice booms from behind the

boys. "You're welcome to have it if you want to pay the real estate taxes, wise guy!"

"Who you callin' wise—" Steve spins around and comes face-to-face with Denny.

The man forces a smile.

"Denny Clay," he says, extending a hand.

Steve looks at it but does not shake it.

"I'm Russell's father and this is our property," Denny continues. "Can I help you?"

Steve puffs out his chest and takes in the surroundings.

"So, you live in this junkyard? That's lame."

"Actually, it's a vintage salvage depot for the discriminating nostalgist."

Steve, Joey, and Johnny exchange looks. Johnny scratches his head.

"I think you need to use smaller words, Dad," Russell says, getting up off the ground.

Denny stands by his son and offers, "So unless you're here to make a purchase, I'm going to have to ask you to leave."

Steve clears his throat and hawks a wad of phlegm onto the dirt.

"Let's bounce, guys," he says to his friends. "This place sucks anyway."

As the three teens turn to walk away, Joey stops in his tracks. He runs over to the left side of the yard and readjusts his glasses.

"Whoa!" he shouts. "Maybe this place doesn't suck after all. *Look!*"

Joey points to something in the distance. Steve and Johnny run over to him while Denny and Russell follow his gaze.

"Whoa!" Johnny repeats. "That's *awesome*."

At that moment, both father and son realize what the teenagers are gawking at, but it is too late. The secret is out.

"Oh no," they cry. "Grimlock!"

Chapter 4

Russell and Denny run after Steve, Joey, and Johnny. The three teens clamor around the dinobot and stare in awe.

"Check it out, dude. That thing is ah-*mazing*!" Joey shouts.

"What is it?" Johnny asks.

"Oh, that?" Russell says nonchalantly. "That is a leftover prop from a Japanese monster movie. No big deal, really."

Steve walks around Grimlock, inspecting him from top to bottom.

"Did you say Japanese monster movie?" he asks. "The correct term is *kaiju*, and I've seen each one twice. This guy isn't in any of them."

"Are you sure?" Russell asks, trying to remain calm.

"I'm positive," Steve sneers. "I take my monster movies very seriously."

Suddenly, a voice echoes from inside the trash can.

"*Kaiju*—the Japanese word that translates to 'strange creature,'" Fixit says.

Steve whirls around in confusion.

"What did you say?" he asks Denny.

Russell panics and looks at his dad.

"I picked this *strange creature* up when I was in Japan," Denny says. "It was made in a little village named Cybertron."

"Cyber-what?" says Joey.

"That's not a real place," adds Johnny.

"Oh, it is," Denny continues. "But it's so small it's not even on the map. Good luck finding it!"

"What*ever*, garbage man," Steve scowls.

Joey walks around Grimlock this time.

"Actually, he looks more like a dinosaur," the bespectacled boy observes.

"Aw, yeah," says Johnny. "Like from one of those movies about a theme park where humans clone dinosaurs and they run amok and start eating people. I love that stuff!"

"Only this one looks more fake," Joey says.

Grimlock narrows his optic sensors in anger.

Steve walks around Grimlock a second time, kicking the dinobot's plating with his steel-toed boots.

CLANG!

CLANG!

Grimlock tries really hard not to laugh because the kicks tickle.

"Hmm. Feels fake, too," says Steve.

All of a sudden, Grimlock catches a glimpse of the tattoo on Steve's shoulder. It is of a cat wearing an astronaut suit.

The dinobot has an irrational fear of

felines, and a space cat is especially horrifying!

Grimlock roars in fear, waving his arms and stomping his feet.

"SPACE CAT! AAAARGH!"

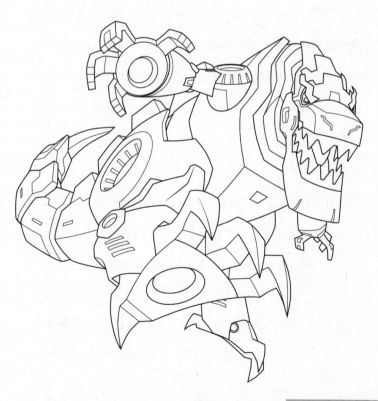

Steve lets out a high-pitched scream and falls on his backside.

"Who turned it on?" he shrieks as Grim-lock continues to flail in fear.

The terrified teen jumps up and turns to run, but he bumps into Joey and knocks the redhead's glasses off—just in time for Johnny to tumble over Joey and trip Steve backward into an empty refrigerator.

THUMP!

THUD!

"You break it, you buy it." Russell laughs.

Denny calms Grimlock down and guides him toward the command center.

Joey and Johnny lift Steve out of the fridge, and they run into the parking lot.

"You better watch your back, junkboy," Steve threatens.

He leans on the hood of a nearby red sports car to catch his breath.

"I think you should watch yours," Russell replies.

Suddenly, the car's lights turn on and the horn blares, scaring the teens again.

It's really Sideswipe!

The Autobot revs his engine.

VRROOM! VRROOM!

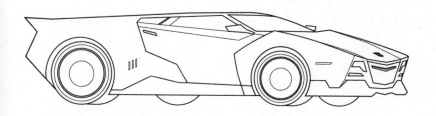

"Gah!" Johnny screams. "This is just like that movie where a guy's car comes to life and starts killing people. *That* car was red, too!"

"Will you shut up already?" Steve shouts.

Following Sideswipe's cue, Bumblebee and Strongarm turn on their lights and rev their engines, too.

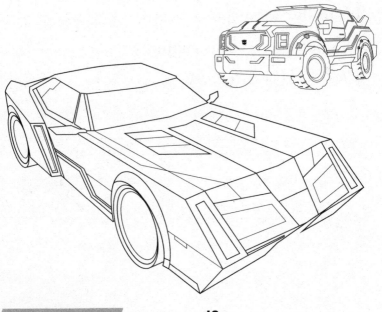

"I think this place is haunted," Joey says, trembling.

Sideswipe blasts a heavy-metal song from his speakers. Steve and his friends cover their ears and run out of the scrapyard.

Russell and Denny are laughing so hard they can barely keep themselves up.

Sideswipe changes into his bot mode and joins the humans.

"What a bunch of klutz-o-trons," he replies.

"Thanks for watching my back," Russell says to the Autobot. "I appreciate it. Those guys are jerks."

"Don't mention it, pipsqueak," Sideswipe says.

Bumblebee and Strongarm shift into their bot modes as well.

"That was a good strategic move you pulled back there," Bumblebee says to Sideswipe. "We backed you up because we trusted your decision. That's how a team works together."

Sideswipe turns away because he is moved by his leader's words.

"I believe he's blushing, sir," Strongarm says with a smile.

"All right, all right, that's enough," Sideswipe hollers. "Isn't there some lesson Bee should be droning on about?"

Bumblebee brightens.

"Sideswipe, that's another excellent idea! You're knocking them out of the park today!"

Strongarm sidles up next to her lieutenant.

"Yes, more training exercises and field-work," she states. "That way, we'll be prepared to trounce our Decepticon enemies."

"I admire your enthusiasm, cadets!" Bumblebee says. "Let's head to the command center."

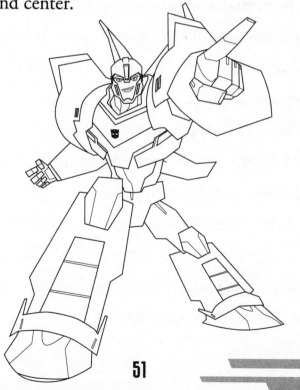

As Bumblebee and Strongarm walk away, Sideswipe hangs back and leans over to Russell.

"Looks like Strongarm may have competition for the position of teacher's bot, heh heh!"

Back at the command center, Fixit uses the holo-scroll to detect any traces of Decepticons. He works his digits over the keyboard and a three-dimensional map of Crown City appears.

A bright red dot starts blipping in an area southwest of the scrapyard.

"This area has a high constellation... constipation...concentration of Decepticons!" Fixit says, chucking himself. "It is near the Crown City harbor."

"Those look like the docks," Denny says. "There's nothing out there but abandoned warehouses."

"A perfect hiding spot for fugitives," Bumblebee replies. "We can boot up the Groundbridge and catch them by surprise."

He attempts a rallying cry that will bring his team of Autobots together.

"Let's move it or lose it, team!"

Sideswipe cringes.

"Not bad," he says. "That was your best one yet, Bee!"

"Stop kissing rear bumper!" Strongarm shouts at Sideswipe and huffs off.

Bumblebee looks out toward the setting sun on the horizon and implores the guidance of his wise and fallen leader. "Oh, Optimus Prime...help us keep it together!"

Then he rushes toward the teleportation device.

Chapter 5

Meanwhile, across Crown City in a more industrial part of town, Steeljaw is lying low in the old steel mill that serves as his hideout.

This cold, calculating criminal was the most dangerous Decepticon aboard the *Alchemor*. Once it crash-landed, Steeljaw made a hasty escape. The wolflike warrior also deactivated the glowing Decepticon symbol on his body so as not to be tracked.

Steeljaw soon began recruiting fellow Decepticons for a much darker purpose. With him now are two of his more cunning cohorts, Thunderhoof and Underbite.

"Nothing must distract us from annihilating those disgusting Autobots forever," Steeljaw says. "Then *we* will be the only powerful beings on this wretched rock!"

"Aw yeah!" Underbite cheers. "More power gets me pumped!"

The canine Chompozoid flexes his metallic muscles and admires himself in a nearby reflective surface. "Let's bring on the bruises, boss!"

"Hrrmph!" Thunderhoof snorts. "Back on Cybertron, *I* was the boss! Had me my own criminal enterprise. I was running an empire, see?"

Underbite covers his audio receptors.

"Oh, not this again," the gargantuan gearhead groans. "How many times we gotta hear the same thing? *I was running an empire*, wah, wah, wah!"

"As many times as it takes for youse guys to get it through your thick heads!" Thunderhoof snaps.

Quick as a flash, Steeljaw leaps through the air and pins Thunderhoof to the wall.

ROAR!

THUD!

"Perhaps you should stop running your mouth, if you know what's best for you," Steeljaw threatens.

He bares his razor-sharp claws and brings them close to Thunderhoof's snout. They glint in the light. The elk-like Decepticon trembles, and his antlers rattle against each other.

"Fight! Fight! Fight!" Underbite chants.

Steeljaw shoots him a deadly stare.

Underbite stops chanting.

"As much as I despise you both, you have traits that will prove helpful in achieving my ultimate goal—coming into contact with the Anti-Spark! With *it* in my possession, I will bring about unimaginable destruction!"

Steeljaw releases Thunderhoof from his viselike grip.

"Sure thing, Steeljaw," Thunderhoof wheezes. "We'll do things your way..."

Steeljaw walks away.

Once he is out of earshot, Thunderhoof adds, "...for now."

Then the elkbot trudges toward the exit.

"Where are you going?" Underbite asks.

"What's it to ya, huh?" Thunderhoof replies. "I'm gettin' me some fresh air."

"I'll join you," Underbite offers.

"Fine, but keep yer yap shut."

Underbite silently follows Thunderhoof outside. After a few moments of walking through a dark alley, the terrible twosome arrives at the docks.

Thunderhoof breaks the silence.

"That Steeljaw's got motor oil for brains if he thinks I can't run an operation," he says. "You wanna know somethin', kid? When I first got to this backwater planet I was runnin' myself a pretty sweet racket."

"What did you do?" Underbite asks.

"You ain't gonna believe this," Thunderhoof says with a smile. "I convinced a buncha

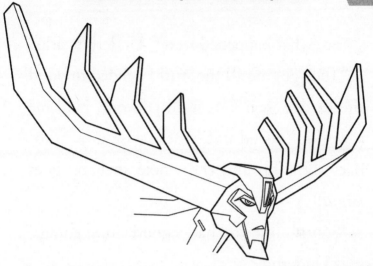

local yokels to help me build a Space Bridge! Made 'em think I was this legendary monster givin' out orders, see? Called myself 'the Kospego.' What a riot!

"What's a Kospego?"

"Who gives a scrap? You had to see these fellas runnin' around callin' themselves 'antler-heads' or somethin'!"

Thunderhoof doubles over with laughter.

"So, what happened next?" Underbite asks.

"They got me all the stuff I needed to build the Bridge, see? Got it all laid out. Had me a workin' portal until these wise-guy Autobots show up and the whole shebang goes *kaput*!"

"Sounds like you had a good thing going," says Underbite.

"Ain't that the truth. And I would have gotten away with it, too, if it weren't for those meddling bots!"

Thunderhoof kicks an empty oil drum clear across the dock.

CLANG!

"Yo!" Underbite howls. "That was a perfectly good snack!"

The canine robot bounds over to the

dented oil drum and picks it up. Then he rips it in half with his bare paws and bites down on one of the pieces.

CHOMP!

The bot's body starts to shimmer and grow. Being a Chompozoid means that Underbite can grow in size and strength by consuming metal.

"Mmm. It's still got some oil in it for extra flavor!" he says, licking his maw. "You want some?"

"Nah," Thunderhoof replies.

"Good," Underbite says. "More for me!"

All of a sudden, there is a loud, clattering commotion coming from within the warehouse.

BAM!

BANG!

CLANG!

Underbite stops eating and sniffs the air.

"Smells like trouble," he says, swallowing the remains of the oil drum. His body shimmers and grows a little bit more.

"Let's get some eyes on the situation before we step in it," Thunderhoof advises.

The elkbot gallops and leaps high into the air. He lands on the roof of the warehouse and waits for Underbite to climb up the side of the wall.

Together, the Decepticons make their way over to a large skylight and peer into the warehouse. One overhead lamp provides the only light. There is movement coming from within.

Thunderhoof and Underbite are able to see three figures: Two of them are lugging large steel drums while the third supervises. There are rows and rows of metal shelves lining the floor of the warehouse. The two figures carrying the drums disappear behind a large shelf. This one is stacked high with several identical steel drums.

"Hmm," Thunderhoof muses. "Seems like we ain't the only game in town. Looks like these players are runnin' a racket of their own."

The remaining figure steps out of the shadows into the moonlight. Underbite gasps.

"It's a catbot!" he snarls. "Catbots are our sworn enemies! *Grrr!*"

Thunderhoof says, "I think it's time for a hostile takeover. What say we drop in with a little welcome wagon?"

Underbite nods his massive head in agreement and the Decepticons smash through the skylight into the warehouse.

SKEESH!

The catbot's audio receptors perk up, and she whirls in time to see the two Decepticons fall into view. Her claws extend and her back arches.

"Did we catch you at a bad time?" Thunderhoof sneers.

"You've just crossed this black catbot's path," she hisses. "Which means *you're* in for some bad luck!"

Chapter 6

Just as suddenly, **two more Decepticons** come rushing from the other end of the warehouse. One of them is a raticon. The other, a weaselbot.

"What's the glitch, boss?" the weaselbot asks, twitching his whiskers.

"Seems like we got uninvited guests," squeaks the raticon.

"*Boss?*" Thunderhoof says.

The antlered Decepticon changes his tune and lays on the charm. "*I* was a boss back on Cybertron. Maybe you hearda me? I'm Thunderhoof."

The catbot lowers her claws.

"I'm Slink," she replies. "And your name don't ring no bell to me."

"You sure about that? I'm a pretty big deal," Thunderhoof says, puffing up his chest.

"Look, moose. You heard the lady," the weaselbot says. "Your name don't ring no bell. So make tracks before we wring *you* out personally."

The raticon swings his tail from side to side and narrows his beady little optics.

Thunderhoof grits his teeth but maintains his cool.

"And who might *you* be?"

"I'm Sneak," says the weaselbot.

"I'm Snitch," says the raticon.

"And I'm the Devourer of Nuon City!" growls Underbite.

"Easy, will ya," Thunderhoof scolds. "You ain't helping."

Slink hisses at the Chompozoid.

"Why don'tcha keep that mutt on a leash?" she says.

"That's it, catbot! You're about to lose four of your nine lives!"

Slink steps back and whistles.

"Boys? Sic 'em!"

In an instant, the two Decepticon lackeys leap into action, springing toward Underbite. They slam him backward, each bot pinning one of his arms to the wall.

"Looks like it's time for me to take out *my* boys," Underbite grunts. He flexes his bulging biceps and breaks free from Snitch and Sneak.

"Meet Thundercruncher!" cries the Chompozoid as he winds up a right uppercut.

BANG!

Sneak goes sailing through the air and crashes into a metal shelving unit.

CLANG!

Underbite kisses his right bicep and says, "Thanks, Thundercruncher." Then he turns to face Sneak.

"Meet Boltsmasher!" shouts the Chompozoid, and he swings his left fist at the raticon.

Snitch surprises Underbite and drops low to the ground. He swings his large tail in an arc and sweeps the Chompozoid off his feet.

Underbite lands hard.

THUD!

"Keep the introductions to yerself!" Snitch sneers.

At that moment, Sneak recovers and pounces on Underbite. Snitch joins him and the two Decepticons slash and bash the big Chompozoid.

"Two bots are better than one!" Sneak cheers.

Underbite lifts each of his opponents by the neck and slams their heads together.

KLONK!

"They sure are!" he retorts.

Meanwhile, outside the abandoned factory, there is a burst of bright, colorful light signaling the opening of a portal. Team Bee steps out of the Groundbridge, and the brightness disappears as soon as it closes.

Bumblebee surveys the surroundings. The industrial area is a large maze of tall concrete buildings. The full moon provides some light, its reflection skittering across the rippling waves of the water beyond the docks.

The stillness allows Bumblebee's thoughts to catch up to him. His new role as leader is at times uncomfortable and frustrating.

Something shifts along the water's surface and takes a familiar shape. Curious, Bumblebee peeks over the side of the dock and looks down to see the reflection of his fallen leader.

"Optimus," he whispers warily. "Is that you? Got any advice on how to lead a group with no military training whatsoever? I'm just wingin' it here, and every time I think they've learned how to work together, they start bickering and fall apart."

The reflection ripples but remains unmoving. Bumblebee can hear the Prime's voice in his head.

You were once as inexperienced as your teammates, and yet your limitless potential has surpassed my greatest expectations. I see the same dynamic spark within your team. You are a leader, Bumblebee, and you have made me proud.

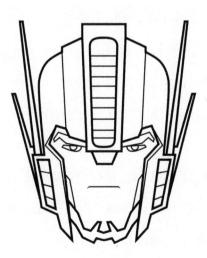

Suddenly, the Autobot feels a hand on his shoulder.

"Optimus? Oh, hey, Grimlock," Bumblebee says, embarrassed. "Must've drifted off. Sorry."

"Seems quiet," the dinobot whispers. "Are we in the right place?"

"*Too* quiet if you ask me," Bumblebee replies. "But these are the coordinates Fixit gave us. Let's look around."

The Autobot and his team walk toward the warehouse.

"We should set up a perimeter," Strongarm says.

"Excellent idea, cadet," Bumblebee replies.

"I was *just* gonna say that!" says Sideswipe.

Strongarm rolls her optics.

"We should enter from the back door," Sideswipe continues. "Catch them by surprise."

"We should drop in from the roof," Strongarm offers. "An aerial view would allow us to acquire the targets faster."

"Both are viable options," Bumblebee replies. "So we'll split up into pairs and double our chances at capturing these criminals."

Suddenly, the warehouse wall erupts in an outward explosion.

KA-BLAM!

Bumblebee, Sideswipe, Strongarm, and Grimlock jump back and shield themselves from the flying debris.

The large projectile that caused the explosion has now landed on the dock with a ground-shaking thud.

It is their familiar foe Underbite engaged in a raging battle with two unidentified Decepticons!

WHAM!

BAM!

The Chompozoid grabs one of the Decepticons by his long tail and whips him through the gaping hole in the wall. The other Decepticon tackles Underbite from behind, and they both tumble back into the warehouse.

"Or..." Grimlock says, peeking in after them, "we find out what's behind door number three!"

Chapter 7

Team Bee stealthily enters the warehouse, prepared for anything but the contradictory tableau before them.

While Underbite continues fighting with Snitch and Sneak, Thunderhoof casually converses with Slink.

"I see you're a fellow entrepreneur," he says, sliding his arm around her.

"Cut the scrap, antler-head," Slink snaps. She wriggles out of Thunderhoof's embrace.

"I got here first. Fair and square. If you *had* marked this territory, I woulda smelled your stench from a mile away!"

"Listen up, sweet-bot, this here is *my* territory. So if youse wanna conduct business 'round these parts, youse play by *my* rules. I'm the boss! And I get a cut of yer profits."

"Not a chance," Slink says.

Thunderhoof snorts loudly, exhaling steam from his snout. "Well, then, I guess we do this the hard way. No more Mr. Nice-Bot!" he shouts.

He lunges at Slink and grabs her.

"Stand down, Thunderhoof!" a booming voice echoes through the warehouse.

The commotion stops, and all the Decepticons turn to see Bumblebee and his team standing in front of the broken wall, heroically silhouetted against the full moon.

Strongarm has her blaster aimed at the elkbot.

"You're under arrest!" she commands.

"Scrud!" cries Snitch. "It's the law-bots!"

"Everybot put your hands where I can see them," Bumblebee orders. "NOW!"

Thunderhoof raises Slink into the air and uses her as a shield. The catbot kicks at her captor, but his grip is too strong.

"Mine are right here, law-bots," he taunts.

"But don't any of youse go makin' no sudden moves or nothin', 'cuz I'll crush her intake valve."

Underbite follows suit and grabs his opponents in each fist. Snitch and Sneak squirm and tremble in the massive mitts of the Chompozoid.

Strongarm puts Thunderhoof in her sights. "I have a clear shot, Lieutenant," she whispers to Bumblebee.

"Hold back," he replies.

Strongarm lowers her weapon.

"Smart bot," Thunderhoof says. "I'm the boss, see, and this is how things are gonna go down. Me and Underbite are gonna trade youse these here punk junk-bots for a free ride, *capiche?*"

"None of you are leaving the premises unless it is in a stasis pod," Bumblebee states.

"Is that so?" the elkbot responds. "How's about we cut a deal? I'll even give youse the friends and family–bot discount."

"What's that?" Grimlock asks.

"You get two Decepticons for the price of one!" Underbite roars.

The Chompozoid hurls Snitch and Sneak directly at the Autobots.

SMASH!

Bumblebee, Grimlock, and Strongarm are taken by surprise, but Sideswipe acts swiftly. He shifts into his vehicle mode and rockets toward Thunderhoof.

VROOOOOM!

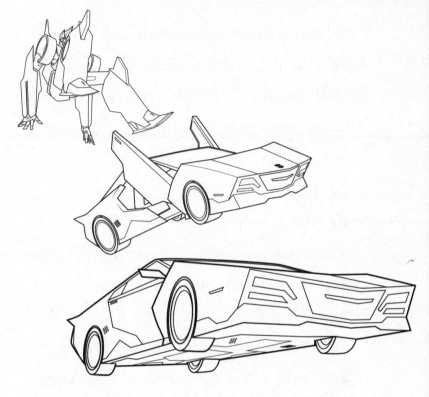

The speedy sports car slams into the elkbot.

BAM!

Slink breaks free and somersaults through the air. The catbot lands on her feet.

Sideswipe strikes again, launching Thunder-hoof across the room, where he bashes into a tall shelving unit. The shelves tip over into the next unit, and the next, causing a domino effect.

CLANG!

BANG!

Tin cans, steel drums, and metal trays clatter and crash all around the Cyber-tronians, creating a cacophony.

"Who's the boss now?" Sideswipe quips.

The other Autobots follow Sideswipe's lead and charge into battle.

Rushing toward the dazed Decepticons, Bumblebee and Strongarm confront Snitch and Sneak with their weapons drawn.

Bumblebee wields an energy sword. The

blade illuminates the dark warehouse with an iridescent blue glow.

Snitch and Sneak shield their optics from the blinding light.

"Arms up, Decepticons!" orders Bumble-bee while brandishing the blade.

"We get the *point*, cop-bot," Snitch says. "Sneak and I are more than happy to oblige. Ain't we, Sneak?"

"Sure thing, Snitch," Sneak replies with a sly grin.

In a flash, the weaselbot lifts his arms up over his head and squirts two pungent puffs of a ghastly green gas at Bumblebee.

FSSSSSS!

FSSSSSS!

"Drop and roll!" Strongarm shouts, jumping back to avoid the gas.

It is too late. The Autobot leader catches a whiff of the toxic fumes, and they cause his neuro-sensors to go haywire. He hacks and wheezes and stumbles, disoriented, through the thick, pungent cloud. With one blind swipe, he manages to catch Sneak with the broad side of the energy blade, knocking him back into his buddy Snitch.

CLANG!

Bumblebee finally heeds his cadet's advice, sheathes his weapon, and changes into his vehicle form. He drives out onto the docks to flush his system with a rush of cold fresh air.

Sneak watches him go and cackles. "I ain't no business-bot, but that seems like the sweet smell of success to me!"

The weaselbot pumps his fists in the air and gives the raticon a high five.

Strongarm wills her weapon to become a double-bladed energy sword. Twirling it with considerable skill, Strongarm brings one end down on Snitch.

WHAP!

Then she whirls it over her head and brings the other end down on Sneak.

WHACK!

Strongarm sheathes her weapon and pulls a steel cable off a nearby hook. The Autobot wraps it around Sneak, pinning the weaselbot's limbs at his side.

"On second thought, keep your arms down!" Strongarm commands.

Before she can get to Snitch, the raticon whips around and hits Strongarm with his tail.

SMACK!

The Autobot gets knocked off her feet.

THUD!

Snitch rushes over to Sneak and starts nibbling through the metal coils with his sharp, bucked front teeth.

"I'll have you out in less than a nano-second," Snitch says.

"Less chat, more chew!" gripes Sneak.

Meanwhile, Thunderhoof pulls himself out

from under the heavy fallen shelf. The elkbot is covered in kibbles and bits.

"Say, what is this filth?" he asks, brushing himself off.

Slink appears from the shadows and purrs, "It's called *pet food*. The fellas on this backwards rock use it to feed something called a *pet*. They all got 'em, and they'd pay their weight in Energon to get their hands on it...were there a shortage, see?"

Thunderhoof shakes his head. "I gotta admit, Slink, ol' gal. That ain't a bad racket."

Slink smiles, baring her sharp, pointy teeth.

"I'm glad you think so, big fella, 'cuz if you wanna be in my gang, you'll need your *own* set of whiskers."

With that, Slink scrapes Thunderhoof's snout with her claws, leaving matching scratches on either side. The elkbot howls in pain.

"Serves ya right, you slimy slag-heap!" she hisses.

Thunderhoof leaps to his feet, but when he reaches to grab Slink, she is gone.

"Come out and fight me, ya scaredy-catbot!"

"Mind if I cut in?" says a voice behind Thunderhoof.

The elkbot turns and comes into direct contact with Sideswipe's fist.

POW!

"Let's dance!" Sideswipe yells. He turns on his radio speakers and fills the air with a bass-heavy electronic dance anthem.

Thunderhoof takes a swing at the young Autobot, but Sideswipe backflips out of the way. He hops onto an upturned shelf and grooves to the music.

The elkbot snorts in disgust and charges at Sideswipe, who halts Thunderhoof's momentum with a swift kick to the chest.

WHAP!

The Decepticon staggers back, then charges forward again with renewed vigor.

Sideswipe evades Thunderhoof's angry offensive strike by leaping around him like a cricket and attacking with a rapid succession of jabs and hooks.

Thunderhoof finally gets his bearings and begins to expertly block Sideswipe's flurry of punches. In a flash, he grabs both of the Autobot's hands in his mitts.

"You got some gears in ya, kid, I'll give you that," Thunderhoof says, trying to catch his breath. "Fast with your mouth, faster with your fists. But you gotta use your head once in a while, too!"

The elkbot rears back and brings his antlers crashing down on Sideswipe.

THUNK!

The Autobot crumples into a heap on the floor. The music comes to an abrupt stop.

"I could use a bot like you in my gang," Thunderhoof says, standing over Sideswipe. "But first, we gotta remind ya who's boss!"

The Decepticon raises his heavy hoof, preparing to crunch Sideswipe's head into the ground!

Chapter 8

BAM!

SMASH!

CRASH!

While the Autobots and Decepticons clash, Slink swiftly packs a forklift with piles of salvageable pet-food cans.

"I better git while the gittin's good!" she says to herself. "Enough of this food fight!"

The catbot scans the area for her lackeys and spots them across the room.

Snitch has finally gnawed through the steel cable that was wrapped around Sneak.

Slink whistles and gets their attention.

"Git yer lousy hides over here and help me!" she hisses.

The raticon and weaselbot jump at attention and bound toward their boss.

During this time, Underbite picks up a supersize tin tub and looks at the label.

"Power Pup Dog Food," reads the Chompozoid. "Lemme try some of this!"

Underbite empties the contents of the tub onto the ground and crunches the container between his paws. Then he chucks the mashed-up metal into his maw.

CHOMP!

His body shimmers with energy, and he grows a little bigger.

"Mmm! I've got the power!" he snarls. "Who wants some of this?"

"Me!" shouts Grimlock.

The dinobot rushes toward the Chomp-ozoid.

"You wanna go one-on-one with the Devourer of Nuon City?" Underbite taunts.

"You're looking at Cybertron's living lob-ball legend, Gridlock Grimlock!" replies the dinobot. "MVB—Most Valuable Bot—four cycles in a row! WHOO!"

"Bring it on, MVB!" shouts Underbite.

Grimlock shifts from dino to bot mode and picks up an enormous steel drum. "Go long!" he yells, and snaps it at the Chomp-ozoid, hoping to knock him down like a bowling pin.

Underbite runs toward the drum, leaps into the air, and catches it close to his chest.

Then he rips it in two and swallows both pieces in the blink of an eye.

CHOMP!

CHOMP!

GULP!

His body ripples with glowing energy, and he grows a foot taller.

SHOOM!

"Thanks for the boost, bro-bot!" Underbite says to Grimlock. "I can feel the pump!"

"Uh, maybe that was a bad idea," Grimlock laments at the result of his actions. "Guess it's time to unleash the Dino-Destructo Double Drop!"

"Let's get ready to rumble!" Underbite shouts.

Grimlock charges Underbite, and the two robots tackle each other to the ground.

Meanwhile, Strongarm recovers from Snitch's attack and takes in the situation.

To her left, Underbite and Grimlock are locked in battle. To her right, Snitch and Sneak are loading a forklift with Slink in the driver's seat.

Straight ahead, Thunderhoof's humungous hoof hovers over Sideswipe's battered body. Strongarm makes her decision. She aims her plasma cannon and fires two shots.

ZAP!

ZAP!

The first blast catches Thunderhoof in the

shoulder and spins him around. The second blast catches him in the back and sends him tumbling over his own hooves.

SPLAT!

Strongarm rushes to Sideswipe's side and revives her groggy teammate.

"Uh...thanks," Sideswipe says as Strongarm helps him off the ground. "Gimme a nanocycle to catch my ball bearings."

"I guess I owed you one, huh?" Strongarm replies. "Now let's regroup and figure out our next plan as a team. We're in over our heads here."

Before the two Autobots can take another step, Thunderhoof appears behind them.

"Youse two are gonna be deactivated right—"

BEEP!

BEEP!

Thunderhoof is interrupted by a honking horn. He turns to see Slink zoom by with her henchbots in the loaded forklift.

The elkbot's jaw drops. "What in the—?"

Strongarm grabs Sideswipe, and the two Autobots run away while Thunderhoof is distracted.

"Don't think I'm letting youse make tracks with my goods, Slink!" he shouts. "I'm not lettin' you outta my sights!"

"We'll see about that," the catbot purrs.

Slink extends her paw and shoots bladed claw projectiles from the tips. The razor-sharp darts zip through the air and shatter the lightbulbs in the overhead lamps.

SKEESH!

The warehouse plunges into darkness.

Just as quickly, Slink shouts, "Get into stealth mode, boys!"

Glowing green lenses pop over the bandit-bots' optics, giving them night vision.

"Not only are they nasty, they're nocturnal, too!" Strongarm observes.

She can hear Thunderhoof stomping around blindly and hurling insults at anyone within an audio receptor's reach.

Oblivious to their surroundings, Underbite and Grimlock continue to tussle and clash, until the two titans crash through a nearby wall.

SMASH!

When they land on the docks, Grimlock

has the upper hand. He is straddling Underbite and pummeling the Chompozoid with his fists.

POW!

WHAP!

POW!

Underbite rolls over and pins Grimlock to the dock. He bares his sharp jaws and says hungrily, "I've never eaten dinobot before. I wonder if it tastes like chickenbot!"

The Chompozoid lunges forward and bites into Grimlock's shoulder.

"YOWCH!" yells the dinobot.

As Underbite lunges for a second bite, he is distracted by the loud screeching sound of burning rubber.

SCREE!

The high-pitched squeal hurts the Chomp-ozoid's sensitive receptors, and he covers them with his hands. He looks up to see a yellow sports car speeding around the corner and heading his way—it's Bumblebee!

The Autobot changes into his robot form and rushes toward the brawling bruisers.

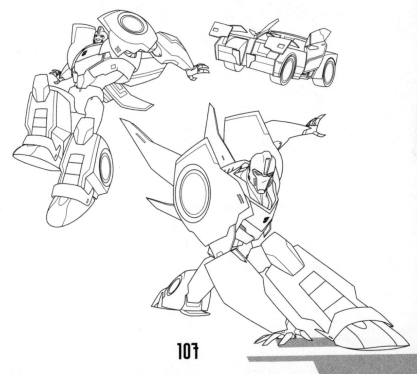

"Biting is *not* a regulated move, according to Rumbledome rules," Bumblebee states.

"Well, I'm ruling the ring now," Underbite growls. He gets in Bumblebee's face. "So just wait your turn while I make this dinobot extinct!"

Grimlock's optics go wide.

"Tap me out, Bee," he says, rubbing his shoulder. "This game isn't fun anymore."

"So how about a little two-on-one?" Bumblebee replies.

"My kinda odds," Underbite sneers.

He reaches for Bumblebee, but the Autobot sidesteps the Chompozoid and delivers a deft roundhouse kick.

WHAP!

Underbite reels back, giving Grimlock an opening to leap up and bring a double-fisted elbow drop raining down on the Chompozoid.

POW!

Bumblebee administers a devastating uppercut that lifts Underbite into the air.

BAM!

Grimlock finishes the four-hit combo

with a swift judo chop to the back of the Decepticon's thick neck.

KA-POW!

Underbite hits the wooden planks so hard he splinters them. With his nose stuck inside the dock, the Chompozoid is momentarily down for the count.

With the moonlight streaming into the

warehouse, Thunderhoof can now make out the shape of the forklift.

"You ain't goin' nowhere," he snorts.

The elkbot's eyes glow red with anger, and steam billows out of his snout. The Decepticon flexes, rears back, and lifts his hoof. Then he stomps the ground hard, emitting powerful seismic waves of energy—like an earthquake!

SHOOM!

The concrete ripples and cracks, starting at the foundation and spreading all the way through to the walls. The building begins to buckle under its own weight.

"The integrity of the entire warehouse is compromised!" Strongarm shouts.

Sideswipe looks up as the ceiling caves in. His optics go wide with horror.

"We better bail before we become a bunch of buried bots!"

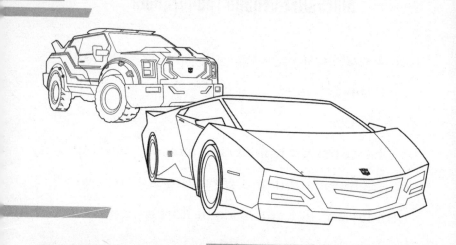

Chapter 9

VROOOOOM!

Sideswipe and Strongarm change modes from bot to vehicle and hightail it out of the collapsing warehouse.

BAM!

SMASH!

Iron girders and steel support beams come

crashing down into their path. The sports car and police cruiser weave in and out of the wreckage until they are finally outside.

The Autobots zoom toward the docks to find Bumblebee and Grimlock standing over the prone form of Underbite.

"Yo, Bee!" Sideswipe calls out. "Burn some rubber, dude. This whole place is falling apart!"

Bumblebee looks down as the dock begins to splinter and crack. Chunks of concrete and metal rain from above.

Underbite comes to and realizes the danger around him.

"This is *way* above my power grade!" he growls, and jumps to his feet. The Chompozoid stumbles toward the empty alley and shouts over his shoulder at the Autobots. "Sayonara, suckers!"

Bumblebee shifts into his vehicle mode as Grimlock stomps away from the warehouse.

The Autobots race toward the safety of the dock's edge.

Behind them, whatever is left of the warehouse finally buckles and collapses into a humongous heap of debris.

FWOOM!

Then . . . silence.

All is quiet once again in the industrial area, where moments earlier a battle raged between Autobots and Decepticons.

"Well that mission was a bust," Sideswipe complains. "Literally."

"There must be a way to still fix it," Bumblebee says.

"You raft...rant...rang?" Fixit asks, radioing in to their audio frequency.

Bumblebee chuckles and says, "What have you got?"

"I've picked up the location of our newest Decepticon targets. They are moving north, away from your location. And they are moving *fast*."

"They sure are some slippery scoundrels," Strongarm states.

"Any sign of Thunderhoof?" Sideswipe asks.

"I'm not getting a reeking…reeling… reading," Fixit sputters.

"Do you think he was buried in the building?" Grimlock asks.

"Good riddance," Sideswipe huffs.

Bumblebee admonishes the hotheaded Autobot. "We can't disregard *any* Cybertronian life, even if it's that of a criminal Decepticon. We can only hope to keep Earth safe until we can rehabilitate them."

"Beautifully put, sir," Strongarm says.

"Speaking of," Fixit interrupts, "the fumigates…fooditives…fugitives are getting away!"

"Send us the coordinates and we'll pursue immediately," Bumblebee says.

Fixit does so, and the bots rev their motors. Bumblebee summons another spontaneous rallying cry.

"Let's burn some rubber, bots!"

"Hey, good one," Sideswipe replies. "I like the way you think!"

As the Autobots speed away, something buried under the rubble of the warehouse begins to moves. Chunks of rock and dirt shift to reveal a pair of gleaming, metallic antlers.

Soon, the rest of Thunderhoof emerges from the debris. His eyes are burning with rage, and smoke billows from his snout.

"Now I'm *really* steamed!"

Chapter 10

The Autobots drive through the mazelike

warehouse district, finally reaching the other
end of the harbor and shifting back into
their bot modes.

Bumblebee sees Slink, Snitch, and Sneak
in their getaway forklift driving toward the
boats.

"Here's the plan," he says. "Strongarm and I will go on the offensive and capture the fugitives. Sideswipe and Grimlock will stay here and block them from escaping in case we fail."

"Roger that, Bee," Sideswipe replies.

Bumblebee and Strongarm spring into action, sprinting down the dock and leaping into the air. Strongarm whips out her weapon and creates a crossbow. She fires an arrow at the topmost steel drum on the lift.

CLANG!

Direct hit!

The drum tips over and lands in front of the vehicle, causing Slink to slam on the brakes.

Bumblebee descends from above, wielding his energy blade. The sword's bright glow

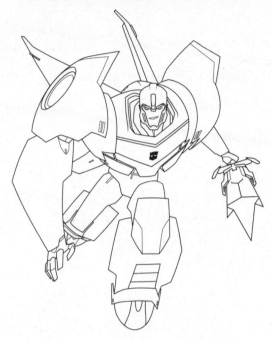

illuminates the night sky as Bumblebee uses it to slice right through the forklift.

SWISH!

"Jump for yer lives!" Slink shouts.

The Decepticons scatter onto the dock. Their escape vehicle splits in half like a chopped melon, its edges smoldering.

"That was a close shave," whines Snitch.

The fugitives hop to their feet, but they find their path blocked by Strongarm and Bumblebee.

"It's the end of the line, Decepticons. Time to face justice," Strongarm commands.

"Let's swim fer it!" Sneak shouts.

"Forget about it!" Slink shrieks. "Catbots hate water, remember? Now make yerselves useful and snuff out those law-bots!"

Snitch and Sneak rush at the Autobots,

but Strongarm is prepared. Her weapon configures itself into a net launcher. Out from the launcher springs a high-tensile net coursing with electricity. It covers the Decepticons and gives them a jolt.

ZAP!

They slump to the floor, unconscious.

Strongarm binds their wrists together.

"Curses!" hisses Slink. "If you want something done . . . you gotta do it yerself!"

She somersaults forward and unleashes her claws, swiping them at Bumblebee. The Autobot raises his blade and deflects the attack. Sparks fly as the opponents clash and slash away at each other.

Slink strikes again, and Bumblebee parries her thrust.

CLANK!

He sidesteps and brings the hilt of the blade down onto Slink.

THUD!

The Decepticon falls forward but retaliates with a jackknife kick that knocks the weapon from Bumblebee's hands.

"I'm afraid our evening has come to an end," Slink says, and prepares to shoot her claw-darts at the Autobot. "Say goodnight!"

"Ladies first," Bumblebee replies.

He grabs Slink by her forearm before she can shoot and hurls her over his shoulder. She lands on top of Snitch and Sneak and gets zapped by the net.

ZZARRK!

"Nice moves, Lieutenant," Strongarm says.

Bumblebee thanks her as Sideswipe and Grimlock arrive, bummed over missing all the excitement. Bee contacts the command center.

"Fixit? The Decepticons have been captured. Whip us up a Groundbridge, will ya?"

The mini-con opens the glowing portal, and the Autobots walk into the light. Grimlock leads the way, dragging the snoozing criminals behind him. Then Bumblebee and

Strongarm enter. Sideswipe saunters behind, bringing up the rear.

Suddenly, the young Autobot is blindsided by a hulking figure and roughly lifted off his feet!

"Oof!"

The Groundbridge disappears as Sideswipe hurtles across the docks and lands on a nearby large boat. Dazed and disoriented, the Autobot looks up just in time to see his attacker come crashing down on top of him.

"Thunderhoof!" Sideswipe grunts. "Ready for round two?"

The elkbot laughs. "There's that fast mouth runnin' off again. Let's see how much you can say when you're sleepin' with the fishes."

Thunderhoof lifts Sideswipe up over his

head, ready to throw him overboard. Sideswipe scrambles to reach his weapon. He clumsily drops the device and watches it roll across the deck.

"Scrap," he whispers.

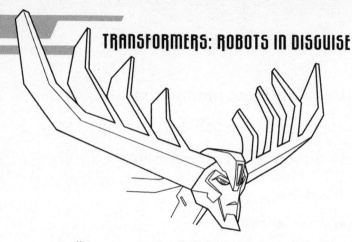

"Bon voyage!" Thunderhoof hollers, and heaves Sideswipe out to sea.

The tough little Autobot grabs on to the boat's railing just in time and slams into the port side of the ship. Sideswipe winces but ignores the pain. Furious, Thunderhoof searches the boat for a weapon and discovers a harpoon.

Sideswipe's optics go wide as the Decepticon advances with the sharp implement. The Autobot's free arm reaches for something dangling nearby.

"Guess I'll have to scrape this barnacle off the old-fashioned way." Thunderhoof snorts.

The elkbot raises the harpoon high when, all of a sudden, Sideswipe stuffs a round life preserver around his antlers!

WHUMP!

"That's enough out of you," Sideswipe quips. "*I* make the jokes around here."

The elkbot drops his weapon and grapples with the flotation device. Sideswipe hoists himself onto the boat and scurries to his weapon. He is outmatched in pure strength and instead decides to rely on his quick thinking.

After an awkward struggle, Thunderhoof rips off the life preserver and howls.

"AARGH! You'll pay for this!"

"Hey, *you* were the one who told me to use my head, remember?"

The elkbot smiles. He lowers his head and aims his antlers at Sideswipe. He charges wildly, intent on spearing the Autobot once and for all.

At the last second, just as Thunderhoof is about to deliver his devastating blow, Sideswipe flips backward and grabs on to the mast.

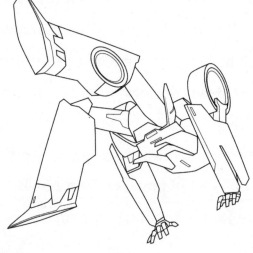

Thunderhoof's massive size and momentum send him crashing through the railing!

SPLASH!

The Decepticon plunges into the depths of the Crown City harbor.

Sideswipe hops down and peeks over the edge. There is no sign of his adversary in the dark rippling water.

Just as he is about to contact his teammates, the Groundbridge reappears.

Bumblebee steps out and finds Sideswipe on the boat. "There you are! Is this your way of getting out of stasis pod cleaning?"

"Nah, I just had some unfinished business to take care of."

Sideswipe hops onto the dock. He tells

Bumblebee what happened with Thunder-hoof.

Bumblebee reacts with surprise. "I'm impressed, Sideswipe! Way to step up your game."

"Hey, I have a good teacher," Swideswipe says, and fist-bumps Bumblebee. "It's gonna be a long walk back to shore for Thunder-hoof."

"Yup," Bumblebee replies. "So let's go recharge."

"Good idea... *boss*!"

The two bots laugh and head toward the Groundbridge as the sun begins to rise along Crown City's coast.

Bumblebee catches a glimpse of Optimus Prime's reflection in the water, and he is

almost convinced that the great Autobot hero is smiling.

"I'm proud of us, too," Bumblebee whispers.

Then the great Autobot leader disappears in a flash of blinding light.